**For my little friends,
David, Adam, and Jason.**

Mike Thaler
illustrated by
Arnie Levin

Lothrop, Lee & Shepard Company · New York

My Little Friend

This is my little friend.

Be careful when you
shake his hand.
He's very small,
you understand.

He isn't very big, indeed,
no bigger than a lemon seed.

He sings and dances very well
and sleeps inside a peanut shell.

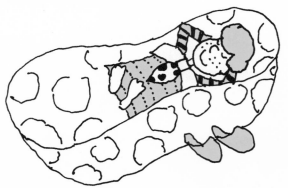

He loves to put on strange disguises,
which he skillfully devises,
then asks me if I know it's he.
I pretend I don't and he laughs with glee.

My friend and I do many things.
We slide down slides
and swing on swings.

When we're in parks
he climbs the flowers
or sometimes we just read for hours.

He tells me all the things he's seen:
the inside of a gum machine,
the closet of a mouse,

the teardrops of a turtle,
a caterpillar's house.
But best of all our fun,
I think,
is trying to make
each other blink.

I make him boats of ice-cream sticks
and he sails out on tour.
I have to watch him very close
or he'll go down the sewer.

He loves to play with clocks and
watches. Of course, you understand,
time is much more fun when you
can ride the minute hand.

We get in trouble sometimes.
Once he fell into the stew,
and then he was discovered
by my Aunty Emma Lou.

Then there was the time in school
when he got in the teacher's hair.
She was very mad at me.
She thought I put him there.

But generally we're very good
and don't make too much trouble,
and life goes by quite merrily,
as easy as a bubble.

He loves to fly on kites
for then he feels quite tall.
He says that from the sky
I look very small.

I've learned so much from him.
I hope he's learned from me.
Once we made a lemon boat
in a cup of tea.

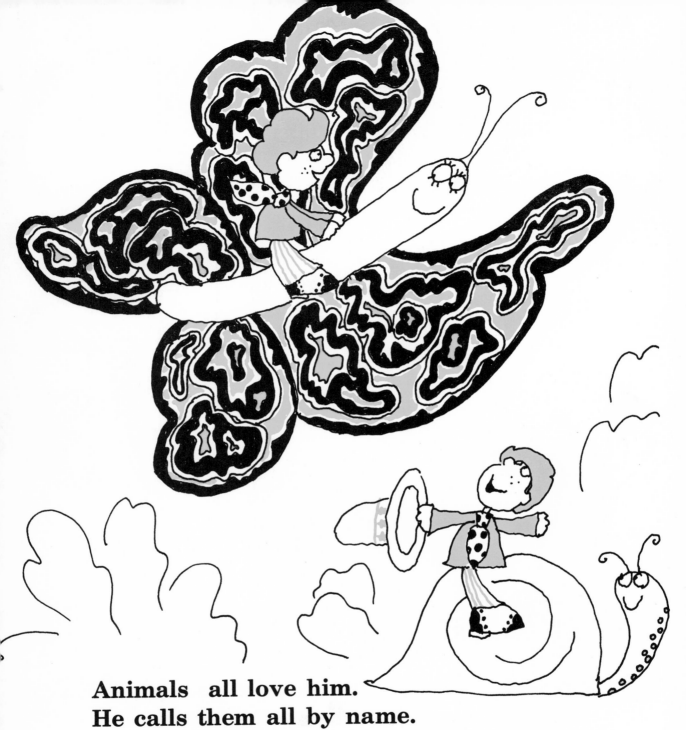

Animals all love him.
He calls them all by name.
Butterflies will give him rides
and snails will do the same.

The day we went to see the zoo
he gave me quite a scare.
He climbed up on the lion's head
and braided all his hair.

He's not afraid of anything:
mountain, man, or mouse.
But when the wind blows hard outside,
he stays inside the house.

He doesn't care for football
but at marbles he's a whiz,
and in a game with other kids
they all wind up as his.

He loves to put on vaudeville shows
and dress up like a clown
and juggle pretty yellow beads
or just stand upside down.

He knows a thousand funny jokes,
and can make a thousand faces.
He fills the hours with happiness
and dances in the spaces.

Sometimes he goes off quietly
and sits behind a pea.
I wonder what he thinks of,
and if he thinks of me.

He always returns then
in a strange and new disguise
and changes back into himself
right before my eyes.

One day he'll be a beggar,
the next he'll be a king.
He says from day to day
we all are everything.

He always makes me laugh,
and chases all my fears,
and says that if I cry too much,
he'll drown in all my tears.

He's been my friend and I've been his
in just this very way.

And we discover something new almost every day.

I still remember how we met—
at least I think I do.
I found him on a Friday morning,
sitting in my shoe.
He asked me if I knew a thing
that would never ever end.

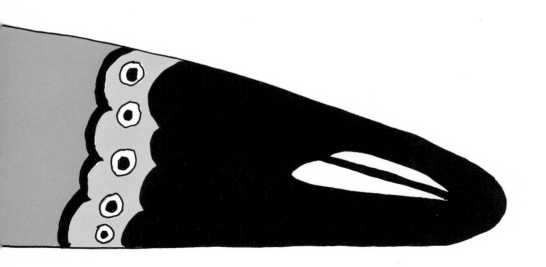

And since that Friday morning
he's been my little friend.